Her Secret Santa

THE SAINTS || BOOK ONE

A. Alatorre, A. Smith, & C. Hebert

For all you naughty girls who like being watched...
be a *good girl* for Santa.

Her Secret Santa

Spotify Playlist

Prologue

BACKSTAGE

"Next!" a man's gentle but raspy voice shouted from the other side of the curtain, ushering me onto the center stage. My hand trembled lightly, as I pushed the thick, black, velvet curtain aside, my eyes blinded by the instant golden stage lights. I moved my hand, shielding my eyes from the warm light. My feet gracefully stepped one in front of the other, the sound of my heels tapping, leading my body to the weathered silver pole in the center of the dark, scuffed stage. Breathing deep, I scanned my eyes from right to left, slowly absorbing the ambience of the infamous Velvet Stag Gentlemen's Club. The entirety of the club dripped with elegance and forbidden passion. Straight across from the stage of the spacious club, past clusters of empty sleek tables sat the large wood panel bar, illuminated by rows of neon lights, burning a low red. To the left of the stage hung a row of heavy red velvet curtains, concealing the club's infamous private rooms. Stairs branched from the side of the stage, leading above the private rooms to a wall of tinted glass that reached across and above the bar. A small, quick flash glinted behind the deeply shadowed glass on the second floor, causing my head to tilt in curiosity. Fingers snapped, drawing my attention to the heavily tattooed man seated beyond the warm stage lights. His dirty blonde hair was pulled into a bun atop his head, a matching beard reaching just past his chin. He was built, with bulging muscles and broad shoulders, wearing a dark tailored suit. Handsome yet terrifying.

"Whenever you're ready." The man's voice was strangely comforting. My heart began to race as my breathing increased, my nerves attempting to take control. *Breathe.* I inhaled slowly through my nose, exhaling through my mouth. *Just breathe.* I desperately needed this job. After everything that had happened, I needed it, and I was going to work my ass off to get it.

My anxiety instantly soothed itself to a calm as I closed my eyes and focused, wrapping my leg across the cold pole as I waited for my cue. The man snapped, signaling for the music to begin as my body remained firmly in position. The sound of static began to softly play, my chosen song crescendoing in the air as the bass throbbed beneath my feet, vibrating through my bones. The song lulled my mind into a trance as my body moved, melting into the music.

THE OFFICE

"I don't understand, why are we *still* holding auditions?" The muffled voice on the other side of the phone attempted to appease me, failing miserably. My temper was already short, ignited by this inconvenience. "How hard can it be to find a woman who can dance on a fucking pole?!" My thumb slammed against the screen, immediately ending the phone call. *This is fucking ridiculous. We should've found a new dancer by now.* I rubbed my hand across my face, then ran it through my raven black hair as the stage lights reflected off the ring wrapped around my tattooed finger. As I turned away from the tinted window toward my desk, the heavy sound of a rhythmic bass began to play from below, pulling my attention toward the center stage. *Another fucking audition.*

I watched the woman move with the music, something about her caught my eye. Her wild onyx hair swirled as she moved gracefully around the pole, her body perfectly in sync with the throbbing beat. Everything about her drew me in, consuming my focus. The way she moved enticed me, a part of my soul hungered to see more. I wanted her. I *needed* her. My eyes remained attached to her body as she danced, breaking away only to send a single word text. *Mine.*

CENTER STAGE

"Stop!" The man's voice cut through the music, shattering my focus as I stumbled. My breathing was heavy, beads of sweat lightly dripping down my face as my hands gripped my knees. *What the fuck?* I hadn't even made it halfway through my dance. My music has been cut short, leaving me clueless as to what happened.

"Excuse me," I huffed, raising a brow, "but my routine—"

"Nevermind that." The man raised his hand, focused on his phone, refusing to make eye contact. "He's seen enough." *He?* My neck prickled as the feeling of being watched shadowed along my spine. My gaze lifted, glancing across the club up at the tinted glass. My eyes caught sight of a faint silhouette watching from above. Who was stalking behind the dark glass?

"You should head backstage and join the other girls. Get yourself a water." The man remained glued to his phone, his face lighting up as he typed. "I'll be back in a minute."

A tsk of annoyance escaped my mouth as I straightened my back. My heels clacked with attitude as my feet led me to the curtain back behind the stage and into the dressing room. The other auditioning dancers were lounging around in brightly-colored attire, waiting for feedback on their auditions. They glared at me as their low, gossiping whispers danced through the room, following me as I quietly made my way to the back. I caught a glimpse of my sweaty reflection in the vanity mirror. Quickly, I pulled a small towel from my bag, wiping my face as I tried to hide my mouth, hoping not to draw unwanted attention to the large scar across the edge of my lips.

Staring at my reflection, I watched as the same man from before stepped through the curtains and cleared his throat. "Alright ladies, listen up." The women flocked toward him as I turned away from the mirror, remaining at the back of the group. "Thank you all for coming out today. I personally *really* enjoyed the show. The boss has made his decision, and unfortunately, it is with a heavy heart that I say you are all free to go." He placed his hands across his heart, with a smile as the women collectively scoffed. "Trust me, I hate to see y'all go, but I don't call the shots." He clapped his hands together, giving the dancers a flirty smirk as they grumbled amongst themselves, gathering their belongings. "Have a great night, ladies." He winked as the room quickly cleared. I tossed the small towel over my shoulder and grabbed my bag, following suit, when he snapped at me, pointing his extended finger in my direction. "Ah, not you." The flirtiness in his voice had me swallowing with growing anxiety. The room went silent as we were the only two people remaining backstage. "Bossman wants you to start tomorrow." The mixture of fear and anticipation left me speechless. I was hired. I had a job. He turned to leave, "Oh," he stopped, his inked hand rubbing his jaw as his eyes remained low, "wear black. He doesn't want to see his Vixen in bright colors." His hand motioned to my pastel attire.

"Vixen?" The word stumbled from my lips. *His?*

The man shrugged. "He chooses the stage names."

"But—"

"Uh-uh," the man argued, shaking his head, "trust me, you don't want to disobey him. You're *his* Vixen now." He winked playfully as he exited the dressing room.

The First Day

VIXEN

"This way." The man from auditions opened the front door, motioning for me to step inside and onto the main floor of the club. Despite his harsh voice and presence, his warm hazel eyes seemed gentle, almost caring. I pulled my gym bag close, clutching it harder as I quickly stepped into the club. The sense of being watched instantly returned, sending a small flicker of exhilaration up my spine. "Name's V, by the way." He extended his hand, balled into a fist, with a smile. My eyes glanced from his face to his hand, lightly fist-bumping him. "Alright. Well, you should know where the dressing room is from yesterday. Just head backstage and get yourself ready. We're about to open and you've got the last dance tonight." I nodded as I turned, glancing up at the tinted glass lining the second floor before making my way back to the dressing room.

The sound of chattering voices silenced the moment my feet stepped around the corner into the dressing room. I halted, all eyes on me, my palms squeezing the strap of my bag. I bit my lip as I scanned the small room. my gaze met the eye's of a brunette dancer to my right, sitting in front of her lit vanity. Gathering my confidence and setting my shoulders, I approached her. *Might as well make a friend.*

"Excuse me," I smiled, feeling the scar tighten across my lips, "do you—"

The woman scoffed, looking me up and down, her blatant rudeness silencing my words. She rolled her eyes and leaned closer to her mirror, running dark red lipstick across her lower lip. "As if." The blonde seated next to her snickered, eyeing me through the mirror as my cheeks burned with embarrassment. *Don't let them get to you.*

A soft, warm hand gently grazed my elbow, and I turned to find a welcoming smile from a beautiful woman dressed in neon green. She poked my shoulder, teasing. "You must be the new Vixen everyone's talking about." My eyebrow raised, cautious yet curious as I nodded. "*Your* vanity is over here." She stepped around me, her black, thigh-high leather boots shining in the light as she walked over to the corner of the room.

Her tight mahogany curls bounced as she flipped her hair and tapped the chair. "Come on now, don't be shy." She motioned for me to take a seat. Feeling the weight of the other dancer's eyes, I quickly shuffled past them and sat down. I spied a single red rose and tube of lipstick on the counter, a small red envelope taped to the mirror.

I hesitated before gently peeling the card from the mirror, noticing the darkened looks of the dancers as I pulled the note close. The sounds of their displeasure echoed through the room.

"Ignore them." The woman leaned down, staring at my reflection, smiling. "They're just a bunch of bitches, jealous 'cause he chose you." She winked, her amber eyes sparkling. "Name's Angel, Val's right hand gal. You let me know if there's anything you need." She patted my shoulder. "Especially if one of them gives you any trouble. I got you." She smiled once more before prancing over to her locker.

I dropped my bag to the floor and stared at the red envelope with my chosen stage name. *He chose you.* Angel's words echoed in my brain. I picked up the single rose and brought it to my nose, softly inhaling its sweet aroma. My fingers carefully opened the envelope, pulling a small, one-sided card from within and read the hand-writing inked across the stark white paper: *Don't hide your face. Your Secret Santa.* My hand lightly touched the scar across my lips, glancing at the tube of lipstick. Carefully, I removed the cap and rolled the tube admiring the luscious blood-red color. The vibrant red was once my signature color, before *he* took it from me.

My eyes stared back at me in the mirror, examining the scar, stark against my ivory skin. *Fuck it.* I slowly ran the bold color along my lips, taking my time to ensure perfection, pleased with my reflection.

NICHOLAS

The laptop screen flickered as the live security feed switched to her vanity. I exhaled a heavy puff of honey-tainted smoke as my hand carefully gripped the rim of the glass, swirling the caramel colored brandy within. The image of her leaning in toward the mirror, gliding the lipstick slowly across her lips, consumed me. She rubbed her red lips together. *Perfect.* The scar across her mouth only enhanced her beauty, despite her obvious attempts to conceal it. *You can't hide from me, Vixen.*

A knock outside the office alerted me to V's presence as he opened the door. "You called, Nicholas?" My eyes remained fixated on the security feed.

"The brunette." I pointed at the screen, cigar in hand.

His face twisted in confusion, briefly eyeing the security feed. "Candy?"

I raised the glass to my lips. "Bump her. Give her spot to Vixen." I swallowed down the brandy, its warm, oaky flavor burning my throat, its zesty aftertaste coating my tongue.

V raised his eyebrows and smirked. "Whatever you say, boss." He turned to leave, shutting the door behind him.

My breathing slowly intensified, puffing out another mouthful of smoke as I watched her. Her tinsel green eyes sparkled, complementary color of her lips as she tossed her long hair over her shoulder. My hand tightened, squeezing the cigar, imagining instead that wild black hair threaded around my knuckles, being pulled beneath my palm. *What I would give to ride her like the Vixen she is.*

"Hey, Vixen," V's voice played through the security screen as he entered the dressing room. "Change of plans. You'll be dancing after Angel tonight."

Candy jumped from her chair. "What the fuck, V? That's my spot!"

"Hey, don't shoot the messenger," he smirked. "Boss's orders." He winked toward the hidden camera as he left the dressing room. *Dumbass.* My mouth curved into a small smile.

Candy glared at Vixen before storming from the room after V as another dancer quickly followed behind her. Vixen turned back toward the vanity, blushing as she flashed a faint smile she thought no one could see. The lips curved higher, pleased with her reaction as I took another swig of brandy.

There's my Vixen.

The Second Day

NICHOLAS

My eyes widened as the live security footage played on the laptop, anticipation in my veins. The sound of her steps quieted as her tinsel green eyes noticed the gift I left her—my Vixen. She glanced around the room, noting the expressions of the other dancers. *They're envious that you caught my eye.* She hesitated a moment before approaching the large blood-red bouquet of roses that I left at her vanity. I watched closely as she gently ran her fingertips across the petals before picking up the small red envelope propped up against the vase. My body leaned forward, mindlessly spinning the gold stag ring on my right hand. My eyes were fixated on her expression, noticing the slight sparkle in her eyes as she read my letter. *Red suits you. Your Secret Santa.* The carnal desire only grew as her fingers lightly touched her luscious lips.

The overgrowing crowd of lively men in the club below cheered, signaling that Angel had begun her signature pole routine, unmatched by the other dancers. V approached the slightly ajar office door, knocking as he stepped inside. My hand slowly closed the laptop as my focus shifted. "Do you have what I asked for?"

V removed a file from beneath his dark jacket, tossing it across the desk. "Everything's in there."

My hand slid the file close as I scanned the little information inside. "Is this all of it?"

"That's all we could find. Seems there's some things in your Vixen's past she doesn't want us to know." As I flipped through the handful of pages, the absence of answers fueled my curiosity. "This can't be everything," I glanced at V, sighing as he shrugged. "Keep looking. I want to know everything." *What are you hiding?*

V nodded. "You got it, boss. Let me know if there's anything else you need." I thanked him as he winked, closing the office door behind him.

I tossed the flimsy file across the desk, re-opening my laptop to watch the security feed again. She was preparing to go on stage, adjusting a deep red lingerie set that suited her perfectly. My elbows planted firmly across the desk as I leaned forward, watching her every move. She turned to leave, stopping to smell the roses once more, another soft smile hidden behind her hair. Beautiful. She turned, heading to the stage for her upcoming dance. Watching her walk away, dressed in my color, made my pulse to race and heat to build in my stomach. I leaned back, adjusting myself as my gaze shifted to the main stage.

The music and lights faded as Angel smiled, her neon green outfit glowing in the blacklight as she collected her well deserved earnings. She rose, blowing a kiss to the crowd, overly exciting them as they tossed more cash her way. I smiled, shaking my head. *Always milking them.*

I stood, rolling my sleeves as I walked toward the tinted glass, the stage in full view, waiting for my Vixen. The growing anticipation of seeing her perform fueled me as the lights changed color, setting the tone for her set. The music rolled into her song as a single light illuminated the pole. Right on cue, she sensually stepped from behind the black velvet curtain, smiling as she moved towards the pole. Her eyes scanned the audience, her confidence instantly fading as the music continued and her body glided along the pole. Something wasn't right.

Her movements were stiff, not as graceful as before. Her face showed a glint of displeasure, masked behind a forced smile. Her eyes kept bolting to the audience of unruly men, glancing over her shoulder each time her body turned away from them. My focus peeled from her, searching the crowd below for the cause of her discomfort. *Who took your smile away?*

My gaze bounced between her and the crowd, desperate to know what was wrong. My head leaned toward the tinted glass as a low rumble formed in my chest, my breath fogging my view as my eyes strained to see into the club below. The idea of her feeling uncomfortable ignited my rage as I watched her carry on through her dance despite her obvious discomfort. Time felt agonizingly slow as I watched, unable to comfort her. I impatiently waited as her routine came to an end and the music faded. The stage darkened as the men cheered, tossing bills in her direction, but she ignored the money and quickly shuffled back behind the curtains.

I rushed from the window, quickly checking the security feed of the dressing room on the laptop. She was panting, rushing to her vanity. Her head fell as she clutched her chest, and her eyes immediately shot to the bouquet of roses as a look of disgust washed over her. She snatched the vase and chucked them into the trash, groaning as she struggled to control her breathing. The blatant disrespect angered me, and I let out a growl as I watched her tear my note with raw emotion. *What's wrong?*

I slammed the laptop shut, hair lightly falling in front of my eyes as I headed to the office door. *I need to know what has you so upset.*

As I whipped the door open, V's presence surprised me. "Boss!" He smiled, arms extended. I ignored him, pushing past, aiming for the stairs. His expression turned to confusion. "Where are you heading in such a rush?" He quickly shadowed me as I kept walking.

"I need to see her." My voice was low and desperate.

"What?" V pushed past me, blocking my path.

"Move," I demanded, my voice now a growl.

V held his hands up, waving them at me. "Now hold on, Nicholas. Just think for a moment." I glared at him, flashing a warning. "Tell me, what happened."

"Someone has made my Vixen unhappy and I need to know who." I tried to step past him, but he shifted, blocking my path with his large frame.

"Nicholas, stop and think with the head on your shoulders," he smirked, looking down then back up at me. "I'm not sure having her boss, who she hasn't even met yet, storming into the dressing room is exactly helpful." My eyes met his. "I know you don't like seeing her this way, but think about her. You don't want the other dancers giving her more of a hard time, do you? You know the rules, you can't just go playing favorites. If you do, try to at least not be so fucking obvious."

I released a heavy sigh, knowing he was right. I had already been too reckless, leaving her gifts in the dressing room. The other dancers had already begun icing her out. If I wanted to know what really had her so upset, I needed to figure it out in a different way, without her knowing. My hands rested on my hips as I paced back and forth.

"Tell you what," V patted my shoulder, "I'll speak with Angel, see if she can keep an eye on her."

"Do me a favor, V," I paused, "pull tonight's security footage. Ask around the club and see if there's anyone of importance who may have slithered in." V nodded. "I don't want this happening again." *I won't allow it.*

V smacked my arm, winking. "You got it, boss."

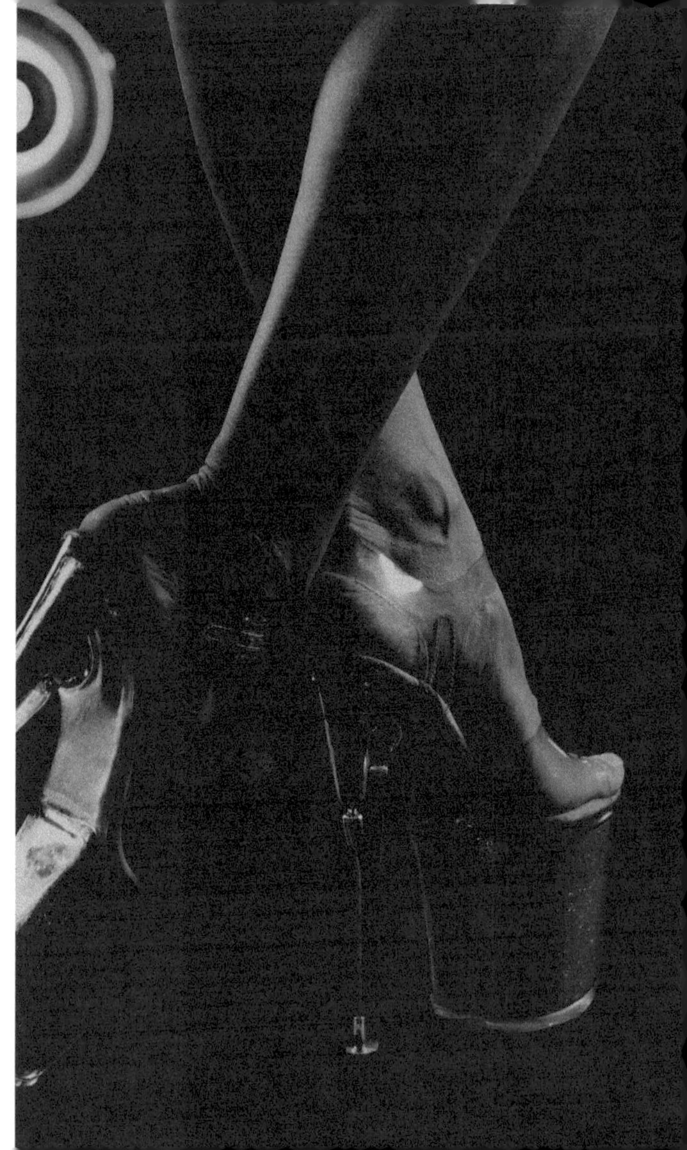

NICHOLAS

"Hey, boss," V placed a small, green tinsel Christmas tree on my desk.

I eyed the ridiculous decoration with disdain. "What the hell is that?"

V smiled. "Aw, come on now, I thought St. Nick loved Christmas trees?" He plopped down in the leather chair across from my desk, smiling as he propped his feet up. I hated that nickname.

"Even our friendship has limits, V." I glanced up at him with a smirk.

He then pulled a candy cane from his jacket pocket, loudly unwrapping it as he pointed to the single rose atop my desk. "And I thought we weren't playing favorites."

I side-eyed V, shaking my head as I carefully began to write on the small card.

He raised an eyebrow as he smiled, the candy cane sticking out the side of his mouth. "Your Vixen's already here."

My hand stopped as my gaze flew to V's beaming face. "Already?"

"Yes, sir. Arrived just a moment ago." He seemed to be enjoying the moment a little too much.

I quickly stuffed the card inside the red envelope, extending the rose and card towards V. "Here. Handle this."

V chuckled, standing as he grabbed the items from my hand, candy cane hanging from his mouth. "You keep having me play cupid and I'm going to bring in an assistant."

"You're not bringing your dog to the club, V." I groaned, lighting my cigar.

"Whatever you say, boss." He winked, leaving the office.

VIXEN

Walking back into the dressing room, I caught V standing at the door, hands behind his back trying not to smile as a candy cane hung from his mouth. I stopped, hesitant of his presence. "You alright, V?"

"*Sleighing it.*" I raised an eyebrow, concerned with his peppy persona. "Someone left this for you." V pulled a single red rose from behind his back and extended it in my direction, beaming with excitement.

My eyes looked him up and down, trying to decipher the reason for his obvious excitement as I slowly reached for the flower. "Thank you?" I gripped the stem of the rose, noticing the small red envelope he handed to me with it. "Who's it from?" V shrugged, prancing from the room without answering.

A weird mix of nerves and giddiness twisted inside as I walked to my vanity and placed the rose down. I gently opened the envelope, the color draining from my face as I read the message inside: *Show me your smile. Your Secret Santa.*

Instant panic washed over me. *Go on, smile for me. Show me that pretty smile.* His words played on repeat in my head as I frantically searched the envelope hoping to find a hint as to who it was from. My heart raced as his voice haunted me—*Don't cry. Pretty girls don't cry.* I struggled to calm my breathing.

Candy entered the dressing room, slamming her bag on the vanity, the loud noise causing me to jump. "Slut," she muttered under her breath.

I quickly tore up the card, tossing it and the rose in the trash. A small tear rolled down my cheek as I turned to face the mirror, my fingertip lightly brushing the scar across my mouth. *Show me your smile.*

"Fuck."

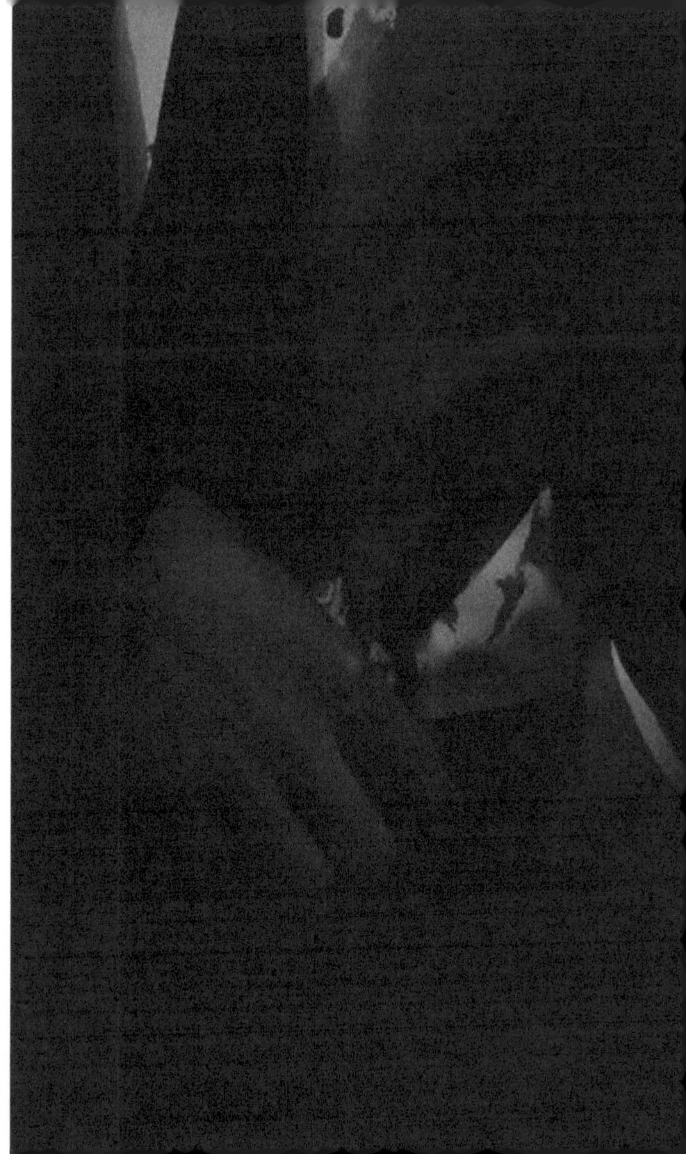

NICHOLAS

V let himself into my office as I poured myself a new drink. He pulled his hair into a bun atop his head before adjusting his jacket. "You rang?"

"Did you learn anything more?" I asked, taking a large gulp.

"She hasn't spoken to the other dancers. No one really knows anything about her." He sniffled, crossing his arms. "Full of mystery that one."

"Have you been able to figure out more about her past?" I finished off the glass, before pouring myself another when he shook his head. My mind had become unhinged lately, obsessed with trying to understand the cause of her displeasure. "Keep digging." My voice turned dark as I stared out through the tinted glass while a dancer moved on stage. "What about our dancer friend?" I asked, chugging another glass.

"Angel? They seem to have hit it off."

"Have her speak with Vixen." I gripped the glass as I turned, meeting his eyes. "Do it before she leaves for the night."

V nodded, pulling out his phone. A chime made his usually cheerful mood melt away as he turned to look at me. "She's in a private dance."

My eyes widened as I straightened. "Excuse me?" V stepped back, fully aware of my temper. "Who the fuck scheduled her for a private dance? I thought I made it *very clear* she wasn't taking those."

V raised his hands, gently trying to soothe the situation. "Hold on now, Nicholas. I wasn't even aware of this until now." He took another step back as the glass shot from my hand, shattering against the wall next to V's head as his eyes widened with fear.

"Where is she?"

VIXEN

My body rolled, moving with the beat as I tried to relax, focusing on the throbbing bass. The Velvet Stag's private rooms were spacious, hidden behind the thick, red velvet curtains and engulfed in pure darkness. The only light provided was from the wandering stage lights that streamed through tiny peeks in the curtain. A hand moved from the shadows of the private room gripping my waist. I chuckled nervously as I quickly moved his hand back. "House rules—no touching." I forced the words with a flirtatious tone, hiding my discomfort. I shook the anxious feeling off as I continued to dance, focused on pleasing him just enough to earn more cash. The hand returned, gripping harder.

I gently slapped his hand back as I spoke over my shoulder, "Uh-uh." The man didn't listen, however, gripping the sides of my waist and pulling my body closer to his. "Easy now," I whispered, fighting his hold. Fear began to wash over me as I could feel his breathing intensify as he struggled to pull me closer and my body leaned forward.

"Stop it." The man yanked me onto his lap. "I said fucking stop!" The music drowned out the sound of my raised voice as he tightened his hold.

His hand gripped my chin as he forced my head to face his. "Look at me," he growled. The familiar voice startled me. "Show me your smile." My eyes met his as my blood ran cold, my body unable to move. The face of my ex, Theo, stared back at me as an eerie smile stretched across his face. His thumb caressed the scar across my mouth, his hand squeezing my face harder as his eyes twinkled in the darkness. "I've missed you," he breathed. A tear rolled down my cheek as he tried to soothe my silent cries. "Now, now," he leaned forward, licking the tear from my skin as I winced in disgust, "remember, pretty girls don't cry." My jaw clenched as my muscles tightened, remembering his painful touch.

Every inch of my body screamed in absolute agony, desperate to escape his clutches but unable to move, frozen in despair. More tears flowed from my eyes as I forced a plea from my lips. "Let go of me." The words were soft and faint, unheard by any. Theo leaned in, brushing my long hair aside as he kissed my neck.

"You know you missed me," he breathed into my skin.

The room began to spin as the music grew, flooding my brain with the painful memories of our past. "Please," I begged, "let go of me."

Theo yanked my head back as his mouth moved alongside my cheek. "Now, why would I do that? I paid for you," he whispered harshly into my ear, "and I'm going to get my money's worth." A scream formed in my throat as his hand roughly silenced me.

The velvet curtain of the private room shot open, partially revealing a heavily tattooed, muscular man. His chest heaved, his piercing eyes glaring into mine, registering my fear. His gaze broke from mine, darkening as his focus turned to Theo.

"You can wait your turn." Theo nodded to the mystery man. "Although, she's got a pretty little mouth if you're up for sharing." Theo smiled, rubbing his fingers across my lips, smudging my red lipstick. "Except for this hideous little scar." His thumb pushed into my scar, causing me to flinch in pain. The veins in the man's hands began to bulge as his jaaw visibly clenched.

V suddenly appeared behind the mystery man. "Boss—"

Boss?

"Weren't you ever taught not to touch things that don't belong to you?" Anger seeped from the man's body as he aggressively gripped the curtain, his arms flexing beneath his rolled sleeves.

"She *does* belong to me." He turned my face, tilting it towards the mystery man as the light flashed overhead, illuminating the scar across my mouth. "See, I marked her. She's mine."

As the sounds of Theo's words drifted into the air, the man ripped the velvet curtain clean from the ceiling, gripping my arm with a surprisingly gentle force. He pulled me from Theo's grasp, our eyes meeting briefly as he carefully moved me behind him.

"V." The deep voice commanded.

V quickly removed his jacket, placing it around my shoulders as he gently shuffled me towards the dressing room, his hand lightly guiding me away. "Angel!" He screamed over the music. "Angel!" V burst through the door of the dressing room, startling the dancers as he motioned me forward, Angel charging in my direction. "I need you to take care of her for me." They exchanged a quick look.

Angel nodded. "I got you, Val." She wrapped her arm around me, pulling me close.

"Everyone out. Now!" V commanded. The authority in his voice startled me. The dancers rushed from the room, Candy eyeing the three of us as she hesitated.

"Get the fuck out!" V snapped as Candy jumped, rushing from the room. V glanced at Angel and myself.

"Go on now, don't you worry your pretty little head about us. I got this." Angel winked with a smile.

The tension in his shoulder eased slightly. "I always knew you thought I was pretty." Angel rolled her eyes as V rushed from the room.

Angel turned to look at me. "What happened out there?"

"My ex," my throat stung as I spoke, "he was here. He requested a private dance, but—"

"A private dance?" Angel sighed, crossing her arms. "You're not allowed to take private dances." *Not allowed?*

"I'm sorry, *who* said I'm not allowed?"

Angel ignored my question, noticing my smeared lipstick. "Let's get you cleaned up." She walked me to my vanity, helping me get comfortable. I noticed my disheveled reflection, the painful touch of Theo's hands on my face making me visibly sick to my stomach, remembering our toxic past. "Here," she handed me a makeup wipe, "clean your face. I'm going to get you a drink." The sound of her boots tapped as she walked to the other side of the dressing room and began to fix me a drink.

My eyes watered as I scrubbed away all remnants of Theo's touch. Raised voices and the sounds of furniture moving pulled my focus towards the direction of the hallway that led to the main floor of the club.

"Ignore that. Here," Angel smiled, handing me a warm mug, "drink this."

My hands gripped the ceramic cup, confused by the beverage. "Hot chocolate?"

She chuckled, patting my shoulder. "'Tis the season. Besides," she sat in the chair next to me, "it soothes the soul." My lips met the brim of the mug, slowly sipping the thick chocolaty drink. Her leather knee-high boots shone brightly in the fluorescent light of the vanities. She was dressed in a tight neon lingerie set that matched the color of her sparkly eyeshadow, enhancing the amber color of her eyes. Her mahogany curled hair lay freely, full of life. She was breathtaking, her presence full of confidence and poise.

We sat in silence for a few minutes as I let the warm hot chocolate seep into my bones. Angel wasn't wrong—the cozy warth calmed my nerves as my body slowly relaxed. I inhaled deeply, closing my eyes as my thoughts recalled the mystery man. *Boss.* That's what V had called him.

The sound of grunts and commotion pulled our attention to the hall outside the dressing room. Angel glanced at me, quickly jumping from her chair. "Stay here." She pointed at my seat, shuffling toward the door. "Oh shit." The surprise in her voice pulled me from my seat, as I placed the empty mug on the vanity and approached her. She raised her arm, lightly moving me behind her.

Just outside the dressing room, V and the mystery man were forcing Theo out the back doors of the club. He was beaten and bloodied, something wrong with his face as he clutched his mouth, blood dripping down his arm. I struggled to see past Angel as she tried to shield me from the scene.

V turned, catching sight of us. "Boss." He smacked the man's back causing him to turn in our direction. Our eyes instantly met. The man was tall and built, with a similar physique to V and equally tattooed. His pitch black hair hung, slightly disheveled, across his chiseled face, contrasting his piercing winter gray eyes. Blood stained his sienna skin, his white unbuttoned dress shirt sticking to his broad, inked chest. He was dangerously handsome, and the sight of him sent a wave of electricity through my veins as he slowly stalked in our direction, V shadowing behind him.

"Everything okay, Val?" Angel asked. V nodded, glancing between the boss and myself. "Nicholas and I handled it." *Nicholas.*

Nicholas quickened his pace, rushing to me. He lifted his right hand, carefully cupping my chin as he examined my face. His eyes stared down at me, full of concern. "Did he hurt you?" His deep, domineering voice melted me. I shook my head, my eyes glued to him. His thumb softly traced the scar along my lips. "Did he do this?" I hesitated before slowly nodding my head. A low growl rumbled in his chest. "Grab your things. You're coming home with me."

"Nicholas," V protested, "do you think that's really the best idea?"

Nicholas glared over his shoulder, my chin still in his grasp. "If he knows where she works, he probably knows where she lives." His eyes returned to mine.

Angel cautiously touched his elbow. "I think your Vixen has had enough testorone for the night. I think she deserves some girl time, don't you think?" They exchanged a silent look, holding their focus for a moment before Nicholas slowly released his hold on me.

"Take care of her, Angel." She nodded, pulling me back into the dressing room. I turned, catching his eyes once more as he watched me leave. *Why was he so concerned?*

We stepped into the dressing room as Angel gathered her things. "Is he always like that?"

Angel stopped, looking back toward the door as the men's voices slowly faded away. "Nicholas? Oh, you know men, they may dress like gentlemen but in reality," she handed me my bag, hers slung across her shoulder, "they're just boys." We exchanged a smile as we made our way to the hall.

VIXEN

My night with Angel had been a refreshing break from reality—exactly what I needed. After a morning filled with casual conversation, Angel suggested we go shopping for new work attire for the Velvet Stag's annual Christmas party held every Christmas Eve.

We had been browsing through rows of lingerie, searching for the perfect outfit, when Angel pulled a vibrant red santa inspired piece from the rack, holding it to my chest. "Here," she grinned, "it's perfect." My hands touched the red mesh material as Angel giggled. "Besides, I hear red is your color."

My smile quickly faded, pushing the outfit away. "I think I should keep looking." My eyes fell to the rack as Angel returned the hanger.

"If something's bothering you, you can tell

me. We can help."

"I never said I needed help." I snapped at Angel. She raised an eyebrow as our eyes met. "Besides, I don't really know anyone here." I whispered the words, slightly embarrassed.

"I don't know your story, but I do know you can trust us—Val, Nicholas, and myself." I focused on the outfits, not wanting to meet her stare, listening as she continued. "Those boys saved me from a dark past, gifting me a future. We've had each other's backs for years. I try to keep those two out of trouble, well, from getting caught." She chuckled. "But you've seen how Nicholas and Val can be."

"Why do you call him that?" I asked, genuinely curious.

"Who? Val? Oh," she giggled, "I told you. We go way back. He trusts me almost as much as he does Nicholas, but those two are damn near inseparable. We're this weird, slightly violent family." She winked. "Granted, Nicholas is a part of a violent family." Her voice fell as she gazed at the lingerie.

I scrunched my brows in question. "What do you mean?"

Angel turned to answer when a blonde haired pomeranian bolted to her side, jumping up her leg. "Milo!" She squealed, scooping the dog high into the air like a child. "I've missed you, sir!" Angel cooed over the dog, rubbing his stomach as he licked her cheek with excitement.

"He sure has good taste in women." V's voice rang through the store as he approached us, catching me off guard with his casual clothes and a dark leather jacket.

A stuck up sales associate rushed to us, scolding V. "Animals are not allowed in here!"

V reached over, covering Milo's ears as Angel eyed the woman. "How dare you say that about my son." I couldn't help but smile at his bullshit.

The woman crossed her arms, furious. "He needs to leave. Now." The door chimed as Nicholas entered the store, dressed in a tailored suit and jacket, hands in his pockets as he neared us. The woman's back remained to Nicholas as she continued to reprimand V.

Angel and V giggled, eyeing behind the woman as Nicholas cleared his throat drawing the woman's attention to him. Her face dropped as if recognizing who he was. "Is there a problem," he demanded in a deep, suave voice.

The sales associate forced her eyes down, her tone instantly quieting. "No, sir."

An older gentleman joined us, placing his hands around the woman's shoulders, smiling as he addressed Nicholas. "Please forgive her. She wasn't aware that you and your associates would be joining us today." He whispered into the woman's ears as she quickly disappeared into the back of the store. The older man clapped his hands together. "Of course you are *all* welcome here. Please let me know if there's anything you need from me." Nicholas nodded to the man as he also returned to the back of the store.

V, now holding Milo, snickered. "Damn straight." He nuzzled the dog close. "Bad enough Uncle Nicholas won't let him into the club." V and Nicholas exchanged a brief look before Nicholas's eyes landed on me.

"Did you enjoy your girls' night?" The question took me aback, and my sight moved from him to Angel who cleared her throat.

"Hey, Val," Angel touched his shoulder, "didn't you need help finding a sweater for Milo?"

V turned to face her, beaming. "Yeah. I wanted to get him a Christmas one. You know, maybe something that lights up—"

"Yeah," Angel cut him off. "Why don't you and I go look for one? I think I saw a place around the corner." V glanced at Nicholas who nodded. Angel looped her arm through V's as they left the store, leaving Nicholas and myself alone.

I forced my attention back to the row of hangers, trying to ignore his presence looming over me.

"How are you feeling?" I glanced up to see him standing closer than before, his eyes filled with a growing concern.

"I'm fine. Why wouldn't I be?" I quickly glanced down at the rack, grabbing a random handful of outfits.

"Why wouldn't you be? You were attacked last night." I tried to ignore his words, turning away, but he gently touched my face, bringing my attention back to his, our eyes locked on one another. "Tell me who he was." His voice was low and demanding. *Why does he want to know so bad?*

I jerked my head away, turning as I made my way toward the dressing rooms. I stepped into the private room, placing the stack of hangers on the hook before I turned around to close the curtain. Nicholas suddenly joined me in the small space, backing me against the wall, pinning me with one hand above my head as he glared down at me. His hair fell slightly in front of his eyes as his breathing became heavy, his voice resembling a low growl when he finally spoke. "I wasn't finished." His free hand brushed my face as he gently touched my scar. "Tell me who he is." The feel of his body so close to mine sent a vibration beneath my skin.

We remained frozen in that moment, Angel's words played in my head. Could I trust him?

"He—" I stuttered as my eyes began to water. "Theo," I swallowed hard as he watched me, studying my face as I struggled.

"He was the one from last night?" His

thumb lightly rubbed my scar. "The same one who gave you this?" I nodded. "Was he who you saw on your second night at the club?" *How did he know?* I nodded again. "That's why you trashed my flowers." He lowered his head. "You thought they were from *him*." *His flowers?* His hand dropped from my face as he slowly stepped back. Nicholas was the one who sent me the notes? The roses? *He* was my Secret Santa?

He groaned, his hand on his hip as he turned. I reached out, grabbing his arm. "It was you?" He turned to face me with a pained look on his face. "You're my Secret Santa? I thought it was him..." my voice trailed off in a question.

"What made you think it was him?" My face fell as I moved my arm away, a dark shadow casting over me as Nicholas stepped toward me, cupping my face with his hands as he watched me.

"The note," I sniffled, a small tear falling down my face, "you wrote—"

"Yes?" he asked, genuinely concerned.

My eyes met his. "You wrote, 'Show me your smile.' That's one of the things Theo used to say to me. What he said to me when—" my voice cracked and I struggled to get the words out as he wiped my tears with his thumb. "It's what he said to me when he ruined my face."

Nicholas's gaze fell to my lips. "I never want to hear you say those words again." He leaned close, causing my heart to jump as he grabbed an outfit, gently handing it to me. "Put this on for me." He pulled away as I glanced down to see a red Santa-themed lingerie set. "I like seeing you in red." Nicholas closed the curtain, smiling as I held the outfit in hand.

I quickly changed into the outfit he chose for me. "Nicholas?" I whispered through the curtain, peeking around to find him leaning against the wall outside the dressing room. He'd unbuttoned the top of his dress shirt, revealing more tattoos across his muscular chest. I cleared my throat.

"Show me." He raised an eyebrow, following me back into the dressing room as he took a seat across from the floor length mirror. I stood sheepishly in front of him, my fingers playing with the fuzzy hem of the mesh Santa top. He lifted his hand, motioning for me to spin. My cheeks burned with a rush of excitement as he lounged further in the chair. He unbuttoned his jacket, revealing a growing bulge in his tailored suit pants as he stared up at me, obviously adjusting himself at the sight of me in front of him. The weight of his gaze made me nervous, suddenly aware of my face. I slowly turned back to the mirror, reaching for the scar when he rushed from the chair. "Don't do that." He whispered roughly down at me. My eyes trailed up at his reflection, catching his hungry eyes as they stared back at me.

A warm touch began at the back of my neck, gently moving down my spine, his metal ring scraping my skin ever so softly. A low moan escaped my lips as he smirked, pleased with my reaction. His hand stopped at the middle of my back, pulling on the satin ribbons holding my top together. Our eyes remained locked, burning into one another. The ribbons fell loose at my side, and Nicholas's breathing intensified as he slowly stepped forward, pushing me against the mirror. I could feel him hardening against me as he breathed into the side of my neck. Our hot breaths circled together, fogging the full length mirror as his veined hands slowly wrapped around my thighs, gripping hard as his knuckles turned white. The mix of pain and pleasure only excited me as I silently begged for more. "My Vixen," he whispered harshly into my ear before biting it with his teeth. I closed my eyes, arching my back into him, fully enjoying the moment.

"Nicholas?" V's voice cut through the building tension. "Where you at? Milo's hungry; we should head out and get some lunch."

Nicholas growled deeply into my ear. "V and his fucking dog."

The Sixth Day

VIXEN

Sitting at my vanity, I began to gather my things when V popped into the dressing room, stepping past the remaining dancers as they headed out for the night. He carefully slid a red envelope across the surface, tapping it with one finger. I glanced up in confusion only to receive a playful wink in return as he dawdled from the room, beaming with joy.

My gaze fell to the small envelope, opening it to find a handwritten card inside: *We're going to finish what we started. —Nicholas.* My face instantly burned with anticipation as I peered at my reflection. Quickly, my hands fumbled to open my bag, searching for the same black outfit from my first dance in his club. The one *he* liked.

As I adjusted my outfit, my mind began to race. The memory of him pressed against me made my body warm and my cheeks flushed recalling his breath against my neck. I hadn't been intimate with a man in such a long time, not since Theo. The idea of Nicholas wanting to be with me, despite my scars, made my heart leap. His words instantly played over Theo's in my brain. I never want to hear you say those words again. I pulled out the lipstick, leaning into the mirror as I gently retouched my face. I was ready for him. Turning, I quickly glanced back at my silhouette, ensuring perfection. Anxiety flooded my veins as I stepped from the dressing room and began to make my way to the main floor of the club.

V stood at the foot of the stairs, smiling with a candy cane between his teeth as his arms lay crossed in front of his chest. I approached him, raising an eyebrow. "V?"

He pointed up the stairs. "Boss is waiting for you in his private rooms. They're behind those tinted windows, just before the office." My head tilted up, spying the darkened room. "Have fun, sugarplum." He chuckled.

My face twisted as I looked back at him. "You enjoy being Santa's little helper?"

V popped the candy cane from his mouth with a smack. "I prefer Cupid. Elves can't grow a beard like this." He winked, stroking his thick, dirty blonde hair.

Shaking my head, I chuckled to myself as I

climbed the stairs to the second floor. My heart raced, my blood boiling with anticipation as I neared the door of his private room. Inhaling deeply, I entered the spacious dark room. The light from the club illuminated his figure, leaning against what appeared to be a large, elegant bed across the room opposite me. "Nicholas?" The door shut behind me, causing my vision to strain before adjusting to the overwhelming darkness.

"Lock the door." His demanding voice startled me as I obeyed him. A sudden burst of light greeted me as the room glowed in a deep seductive red. Straight across the room, Nicholas stood with his sleeves rolled to his elbows, his dress shirt partially unbuttoned as he consumed the sight of me. He was playing with a dark blindfold, leaning against the post of the spacious, elegant bed, draped in silky black curtains that flowed to the floor.

Nicholas pushed from the post and stalked toward me, blindfold still in hand. "Do you trust me?" He circled me, looking me up and down, pleased with my outfit choice.

My eyes met his gaze, finding it filled with a burning carnal hunger. "Yes."

He stopped directly behind me, smiling as he leaned in close, causing me to inhale sharply. "Good," he breathed into my ear. "*Now kneel.*"

I did as I was told and knelt down, breathing

heavily as he placed the blindfold across my eyes, completely blacking out my vision. "That's my good Vixen," his steps moved to the front of me, "but now," his hand grazed my face stopping on my mouth, "it's time to be naughty." Nicholas moved the pad of his thumb across my lower lip, gently dragging it as he groaned deeply. "God, I love these lips." He gently pressed against my mouth. "Now open," he growled. He pushed his thumb deep into my mouth, causing me to inhale, my lips sliding along his skin as he moved back and forth. "Good girl." Hearing his praise sent a shock of electricity across my skin as my hands squeezed my own thighs.

Nicholas slowly withdrew his thumb from my mouth leaving me clueless as to what to expect. The crinkling sound of plastic surprised me, followed by the strong scent of peppermint. He ran something hard and sticky against my lips—a candy cane. Instinctively, I leaned forward, sucking on the pre-soaked peppermint candy as he pulled it back and forth. The candy cane glided along my tongue as he shoved it deeper into my mouth. He gripped my chin, forcing my head up high, leaning down as my throat opened. His mouth met mine as his tongue ran along the candy cane twisting together as a mix of peppermint and euphoria exploded in my mouth.

Deep, passionate kisses mixed with the

sound of heavy breathing and the sound of his belt unbuckling. Nicholas pulled away, taking the candy cane with him as I gasped for air. With my mouth still dropped open, he swiftly pushed his hardened cock past my lips, roughly hitting the back of my throat. My hands reached up, gripping his legs as my nails dug into his thighs. "That's it, baby, breathe through your nose and take it like a good girl." His hands weaved through my hair, pulling tight as I glided up and down, my tongue and sucking at the base, my saliva soaking him. His moans were intoxicating as he fucked my mouth harder and faster, his hips snapping as he drove deeper. His grip tightened, fiercely pulling my hair as the lines of pain and pleasure blurred together. The sensation caused a moan to vibrate up, he jolted in response. "Fuck," he breathed into the air. My hands moved, traveling under his shirt as they raked down the skin of his back. He arched as he came, his warm cum filling my throat, dripping from the corner of my mouth as he pulled away. He wiped the thick drops that had escaped, forcing them back into my mouth with his thumb. "Swallow it." I did as I was told, swallowing hard as the essence of him mixed with the faint remnants of peppermint. "Get up."

Breathing heavily, I quickly stumbled to my feet, using his body to steady myself. Nicholas wrapped his arm around my waist, his hand on my lower back as he twirled me toward the bed. My legs hit the edge of the mattress, and I gasped, gripping the front of his shirt. Nicholas chuckled, grabbing my hands as he pushed me back onto the bed. "Your turn."

The sound of his belt snapped, as though he whipped it from his pants. The cold leather kissed my skin as he wrapped the leather belt around my wrists, pulling them aggressively above my head as they were bound. My lips curled into a smile, as he lifted my legs, propping my heels on the footboard, spreading my legs and baring my lingerie-clad center to his gaze.

The sound of plastic returned as the familiar scent of peppermint filled my senses. His warm hand grazed my inner thigh as he ran two of his fingers beneath the fabric of my outfit; I gasped as they plunges inside me. "Looks like I won't need to wet the candy cane for you." Before I could question his words, a hard tingly sensation replaced his fingers as he pushed the candy cane deep inside me. My body jolted as he slid the candy cane back and forth causing a wet reaction, enhancing the tingling sensation.

My heart raced as he withdrew the hard candy, the slick sound of my wetness followed by a faint sucking. "You taste fucking delicious." My body desperately hungered for more as his lips kissed my stomach lightly, taking his time as he made his way toward my waist. "I'm going to devour you." He whispered the words against my skin, grazing my flesh with his teeth as he kissed my inner thigh. My hips bucked in anticipation as a sudden burst of his breath kissed my sensitive skin. His warm breath mixed with the peppermint caused a cooling sensation inside as the essence dripped from within. My skin prickled and nipples hardened in response as Nicholas shoved his tongue deep inside me. A soft cry escaped my lips as I arched my back in ecstasy.

My throat went dry as my head fell back, my hips grinding against his face as he swirled his tongue inside me, moving back and forth. My hands fought against the belt, pulling against the leather with an uncontrollable urge to run my fingers through his dark hair. I wanted more. I *needed* more.

I lowered my bound hands to his head, tangling my fingers in his hair. Nicholas quickened his pace, unlatching the belt and allowing my hands to freely control him. "Come for me, baby," he breathed heavily against me as he sucked and licked, fueling the fire in my core as he pulled back, replacing his tongue with his fingers. His drenched tongue met my hardened nipples, circling them, my hands still threaded through his hair. I couldn't control myself, pulling his face to mine so our lips met, exchanging fierce kisses between hot and heavy breaths. My body fought the building release, breathing him in my body pushed against his. My legs wrapped around his waist, pulling him closer, forcing his fingers deeper as I silently begged him for more. The tension boiled over as he forced his tongue deep inside my mouth, the lingering hint of candy cane pushing me over the edge. Moans filled the air as I soaked his hand with my release.

Nicholas pulled the blindfold from my face, smiling as he stared down at me. "You did such a good job," he pulled his fingers from my pussy, drenched in my orgasm, "but this was just a taste of what's to come." He licked his fingers, sucking them as his eyes remained locked with mine.

NICHOLAS

"I see your Vixen went home with Angel again," V stepped into the office, his eyes glued to his phone.

"Until her ex is handled, I don't want her returning home." V glanced up as he took a seat in the chair across from my desk, noticing the candy cane in my mouth. Our eyes met for a moment.

V raised an eyebrow. "Since when do you like candy canes?" He smirked.

The Seventh Day

VIXEN

I carried an extra ounce of confidence with me as I moved through my dance. As I left the stage, V winked, passing me on the way back to the dressing room. When I made my way to my vanity, curiousity piqued as I eyed a black box topped with a black satin bow. I was hesitant to open it. A soft vibration hummed from my bag pulling my attention away. My hands rummaged through my belongings to find my phone. I tapped the screen revealing an unread message from 'My Secret Santa': *Open it.*

My eyes glanced around the empty dressing room, landing on the mirror. My phone vibrated in my hand as I read the new text: *What are you waiting for?* My eyes returned to the mirror as my head tilted, faintly smiling. *Can he see me?* The phone vibrated once more: *Beautiful.* My lips pressed together as I smirked into the mirror. I put the phone down and opened the gift box. Inside was the Santa lingerie from before, the same set I'd tried on just for him. *Naughty Nicholas.*

My fingers moved, quickly typing a response: *You looking for another private show?* I couldn't help but smile, biting my lip as his text came through: *Yes.* Before I could reply, my phone buzzed again: *Now.*

"Where?" I giggled. "Here?" *Yes.* I glance at the mirror, realizing that somehow Nicholas could see me. My phone vibrated one last time: *Show me what's mine.* A shiver of excitement sped down my spine as I stared directly into the mirror, pulling the strap of my outfit down.

"Yes, sir."

NICHOLAS

I leaned against the wall outside the dressing room watching the dancers leave for the night, waiting for her. Candy caught sight of me, grinning as she stepped in my direction. "Nicholas," she called, "I was hoping to run into you." Her obvious attempts at flirting always annoyed the shit out of me.

She twirled her hair and bit her lip as she reached for my arm, but my hand moved, catching her before she could. "Don't." Her eyes widened in shock as her face fell, and my eyes shifted to Angel and Vixen as they stepped into the hall.

Candy followed my gaze, scoffing as she saw the focus of my attention as it weighed on Vixen. Pissed, she yanked her hand from my grasp, storming off.

"Slut," Angel snarked under her breath as

she and Vixen approached.

"Classy, Angel." She shrugged, proud of herself, but my eyes remained on Vixen's tinsel green irises. "I need to speak with you in my office." Angel raised an eyebrow, crossing her arms. "You can go, Angel." I glanced back to her, "I'll see to it that she gets home safe."

Angel shook her head. "Sure, Nicholas." She patted Vixen's arm, leaving us alone.

Once we were alone, I stepped toward Vixen, placing my hand across her lower back. A soft exhale left her red lips as I smiled, leading her through the club toward the stairs.

"I thought you didn't want me going home?" she asked as we climbed the stairs and stepped onto the second floor.

I remained silent until we reached the office door. I opened the door to my office, ushering her inside and locking it behind us. "You're not."

Vixen turned, amused by this new game. "Then where will I be staying tonight?"

"Here." I carefully removed her bag, placing it on the ground. "But first," I removed my suit jacket and began to unbutton my shirt, slightly exposing my chest. Her hungry eyes studied me. "You look like you could use a nice...hot...shower."

Vixen raised an eyebrow. "Are you calling me dirty?"

"You will be." I whispered the words as I

grabbed her, squeezing her legs as I heaved her over my shoulder, making my way to the bathroom.

"Nicholas!" she squealed excitedly, kicking her heels.

I slapped her ass, smiling. "Tonight, I make you mine." *I'm going to worship her, making her see I am the one she belongs with.*

My foot kicked open the door to the bathroom open as I flicked the lights on, carefully setting her down on the counter, positioning myself between her legs. I hovered a moment, my hair falling around my face as we breathed in unison. The desire to ravish her grew, burning inside. I had to force myself to break eye contact just to turn the shower on.

As I made my way back to Vixen, I removed my shoes and tossed them aside, admiring the sight of her, sitting on the marble counter in her tight halter dress. I brushed my hair back filled with anticipation. My hands delicately grazed her bare legs stepping in front of her, one on either side of me. She lifted her right leg high, placing it over my shoulder, smiling as I kissed her ankle before carefully removing her heel. I lowered her leg, repeating the motion with the other, continuing to kiss her soft skin. She slightly leaned back, her wild hair falling behind her. She moaned quietly as my hands gripped her thighs, squeezing tight as I yanked her closer to me causing a loud gasp to escape her vibrant red lips.

I towered over her, those bright green eyes of hers sparkling up at me, begging for more. My hand gently caressed her chin, cupping it as I leaned forward my free hand resting on the foggy mirror. I held her firm and devoured her luscious red lips. Our tongues tangled together as her hands wrapped around my neck, gently scraping my skin. She was nervous, holding back. Unacceptable. My hand moved down her face to her neck pulling the nylon straps of her dress free.

She pulled away, hesitant for a moment, breathing heavily through her smeared, gapping red lips. "Don't shy away from me." My hand pulled her thin dress down, completely exposing her chest. My eyes fell to her breasts, excited by the sight of her. *My Vixen.* My control faded away as I pulled her lower back towards me, feeling her nipples pressing into my chest as I passionately kissed her, breathing her in. Her hands gripped my arms as they bulged beneath her palms, struggling to contain myself.

My mouth began to travel from hers, moving to her neck. Her legs wrapped around my waist, squeezing me closer. My teeth dug into her soft skin, her body jolting with a gasp of pleasure. My lips forced a smile, licking the mark I left.

Her body moved, swaying like she did on the

dance floor, inviting me to continue. My mouth moved to her breasts, understanding her motions. I licked her nipple, flicking it lightly, increasing the speed and pressure with each strangled noise from her lips. They hardened beneath my tongue, showing just how much she loved my touch. My teeth lightly clasped around her, a moan filling my ears as she squeezed her nails into my neck. I pulled gently, releasing her as my eyes met hers. She bit her lip signaling that she was ready for more. *Wanted* more.

I reluctantly pulled back, removing my hands from her body as I began to unbutton the rest of my dress shirt. She leaned forward, replacing my hands with hers. "You take too long," she teased, raising an eyebrow as she ripped open my shirt. Her eyes sparkled with desire as I watched her take in the sight of me. Her fingers gently ran along my skin, tracing the patterns of my tattoos. My chest heaved as my breathing intensified, a low growl rumbling in reaction to her licking those luscious lips.

Vixen slid from the counter to her feet staring up at me as she removed my shirt. Her hands fell to my pants as she held my gaze, slowly unlatching my belt and pants. My jaw tightened, obsessed with the sight of her as she lowered herself to her knees, removing my pants with a sensual slowness. *Naughty little Vixen.*

Her bright green eyes stared up at me, aware of how erect I was, fully exposed, on display for her to take in. I raised an eyebrow at the face she made, visibly impressed by my size. My hand lightly gripped her face, pulling her back to me as her palms slid along the side of my bare thighs as she stood. My fingers wrapped around her backside, pulling the hem of her dress, removing it from her body in one swift motion. *Fuck.*

She shifted her weight from leg to leg, visibly anxious. I gently rubbed at her lower lip, caressing her scar as she gazed up at me. I could read the importance of this moment etched across her face. After everything she had been through, I wanted to make this moment just right. I wanted to show her how she *deserved* to be loved. I wrapped my arms around her bare waist pulling her close, my hands cupping her backside. "You're mine. All of you," I leaned in close as my lips hovered above hers, "and I want you just the way you are." Without waiting for an answer, I lifted her up, wrapping her legs around my waist as I carried her across the bathroom.

I stepped into the shower, Vixen firmly in my grip as her legs slowly slid down the side of me. The overwhelming urge to take her became unbearable. I grabbed her face, yanking her hair back as our mouths rammed together inhaling the thick, hot steam. As our bodies pressed together, slowly moving toward the water. "More," she begged into my mouth, gasping.

Smiling, my hand gripped her neck, pushing her body against the cold tile. It bumped the wall beneath the steamy stream, allowing the water to run freely down our bare skin. She arched her back, inviting me to take full control. My hand tightened around her throat, forcing her excited eyes to look up at me, water gliding through my hair and onto her bare chest. "Don't take your eyes off me," I growled, "I want what's *mine*."

Her eyes sparkled, widening as I lined myself up with her dripping core before thrusting deep with one swift thrust. Her breathing hitched, the tight pressure of me inside her causing her body to constrict in immense pleasure. My grip loosened around her neck as I slowly pulled from within, leaving just the tip, hearing her whine softly with the absence of me. My fingers clasped hers, pinning her arms against the cold tile as I forcefully re-entered her, our moans twisting together as I moved back and forth increasing my speed and vigor.

Her panting increased to a faint scream as she moaned, overwhelmed with growing pleasure. I could feel her wetness seeping around my cock, soaking me as her body tightened, nearing the edge. I leaned in, water dripping from my face as I breathed into her ear. "That's it, baby, come." My mouth moved to hers, exchanging a quick passionate kiss as my teeth pulled her lower lip, thrusting deeper, sending her fully over.

Her voice raised as she lifted her head and moaned, pressing her soaked body against mine. The sounds of her climax vibrated through my body pushing me closer to release. "Turn around."

I pulled out before her climax had lessened, fully hardened as she obeyed, facing the tile. My hands grabbed hold of her waist, water cascading from my body onto her as I drove myself back inside. Her wetness overflowed onto me. I bit my lower lip as I shoved her forward, her breasts pressed against the tile as I took her brutally from behind. Her body began to tighten once more, signaling that she enjoyed what I was doing to her. I pulled her body from the tile, my hand across her neck brushing it gently as my other hand reached around caressing her clit. Her head raised, falling back as my mouth met hers.

"Fuck," she breathed into me.

I smiled against her mouth, fully aware of what was about to happen. My pace quickened, chasing her release as mine grew. Together, our breathing intisified as our moans joined in unison, coming at the same time. "Fuck, that's it, baby." Our mouths gaped wide, euphoria filling the steamy room as we continued.

The Ninth Day

VIXEN

Angel and I had gathered our things, making our way out the back doors of the club, when she suddlenly stopped in her tracks. "Oh shit," Angel whispered.

"Everything okay?" I asked, opening the back door, stepping into the alley.

"Yeah, I just left my keys in the dressing room." She tsked. "I'll be right back," she looked at me sternly. "Just wait right here, okay?"

I nodded, flashing her a smile as the club door shut. My mind wandered, thinking of my shower with Nicholas the night before, my finger lightly touching my lips.

"I always loved that smile."

The color drained from my face as my smile faded. Theo. I quickly turned to see him standing across the alley eyeing me with a devilish grin. I turned around, pulling at the club door, but it was locked from the inside. Panic flooded my mind as my hand frantically banged against the metal door. *Please help, anyone.*

Theo rushed at me, turning my face toward him as he painfully gripped my jaw. My eyes went wide at the noticeable marks along his cheeks. "You see this?" He pointed with his free hand. "You see what he did to me? My face is ruined, just like *yours.*"

My heel stomped on his foot causing him to scream, suddenly releasing me. I quickly bolted away from the club, glancing back over my shoulder only to stumble and fall onto the cold, wet pavement. *Shit.* I crawled to my knees trying to get up when a sudden yank pulled me back. My knees scraped against the rough pavement, pain shooting through my veins, my cheek burning as it slid against the asphalt.

"Where do you think you're going?" Theo turned me over, pinning my body down as his knees tucked around me. His hands circled my throat, squeezing with hatred as his eyes burned into mine. "Where's your guard dog now?" He grinned, tightening his grip.

My hands smacked his, trying to loosen his grip as my legs kicked. "Please," I choked, "let—go."

"What makes you think I'd let you go?" My

face burned as I struggled to take a breath. "I just got you back, and you're mine."

"I—was never—yours," I stuttered, my voice strained under the force of his fingers. Nicholas' words danced in my mind—*my Vixen.* "I've always been his." My nails dug into his face with a sudden burst of strength.

"Hey!" Angel shouted from the back door of the club. "Get the fuck off her!" She clicked her keys, her car alarm blaring, alerting the others, as she charged us.

"Angel?" V's voice drifted through the open door of the club as he and Nicholas stepped into the alley shortly behind Angel. The sight of Theo on top of me fueled Nicholas, sending him into a rage as he bolted to my aid, shoving V and Angel aside.

Nicholas yanked Theo off of me, grabbing him by his hair as he hurled him powerfully into the brick wall; the sound of Theo's body smacking the brick was followed by the sound of a wet crunch. I coughed, gagging on the crisp, cold air as it returned to my lungs. Angel ran to my side, helping me sit up as I watched Nicholas.

"What did I tell you about touching what doesn't belong to you?" He glanced back at me. Our eyes met as I nodded, signaling for him to continue. He looked back at Theo, who was obviously terrified of Nicholas.

"V," Nicholas called back.

V removed his jacket and handed it to Angel, rolling up his sleeves as he approached Nicholas and grabbed Theo, turning him to face us. His muscles bulged as he pinned Theo to the wall, extending his arm out and away from his body. Nicholas removed his jacket, gently placing it around me as he bent down, his fingers brushing over my scraped cheek. He kissed my forehead, his lips lingering a minute before turning away as he rolled up his sleeves too. He glanced around the alley, eyeing a rigid block of concrete.

Theo cried as Nicholas picked it up, tossing it around in his hands. "Please," Theo sobbed, "please don't." V pushed his arm against Theo, urging him to shut up. Nicholas stopped in front of Theo, staring down at the block in his hand. "Look, man, she's not worth it. I'll leave. I swear!" Nicholas silently stared at Theo, his jaw clenching. "I swear," Theo sobbed.

"I'll let you live," Nicholas's eyes darkened, "but first, I'm going to teach you a lesson." The sound of bones crunching echoed through the alley, fading into Theo's screams as Nicholas slammed the block into his hand, hammering it into the wall.

Nicholas leaned close to Theo, his voice low and possessive. "You touch what's mine again, I won't just break your hand." He spat on Theo's face, dropping the block. "Next time, I'll *kill* you."

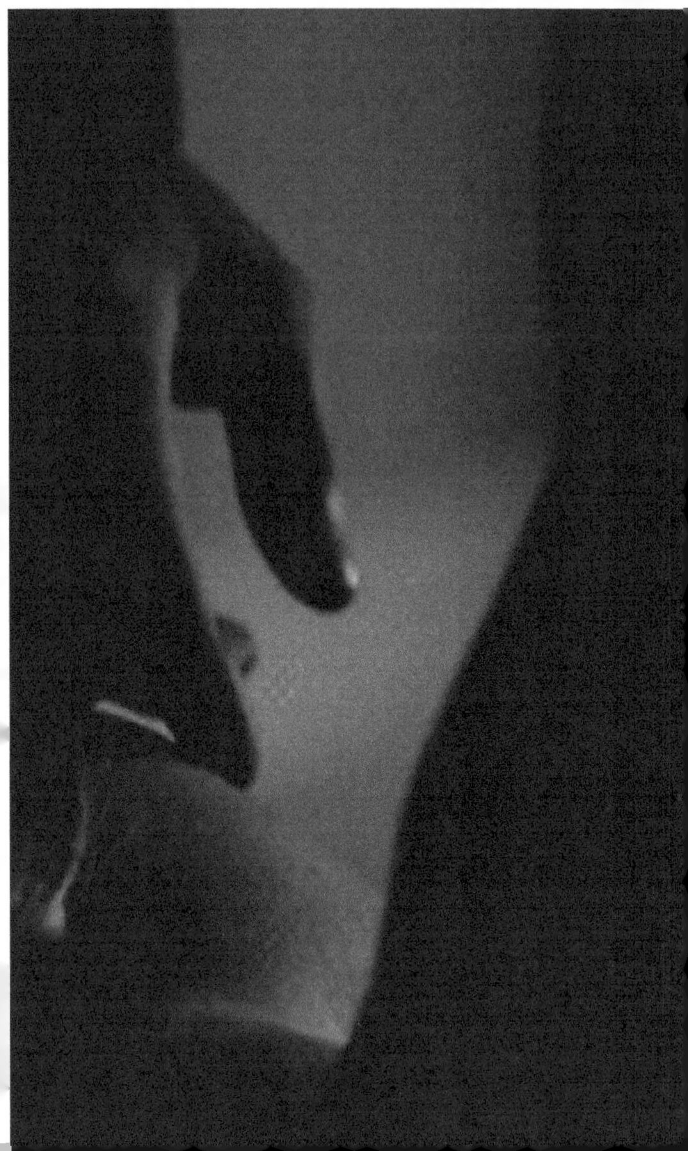

<h1 style="text-align:center">The Tenth Day</h1>

VIXEN

The sound of his fingers typing away at the keyboard slowly woke me. Nicholas was propped up shirtless in bed next to me, his tattoos fully on display. His black hair was ruffled, falling in front of his winter gray eyes as his inked knuckles moved along the keys, a golden stag ring on his right hand. I rolled to my side, my body sore from the prior night's injuries, and exhaled softly.

Nicholas noticed my movement, lifting his right hand as he sweetly stroked my cheek. I winced faintly as his ring brushed against the scratches along my skin. "Did I hurt you?" He raised his hand, concerned by my reaction.

I pulled his hand back, kissing the inside of his palm. "Never." I stared at the golden stag, my fingers tracing the three dimensional shape. "Let me guess, a stag to represent the club?" I flirtingly raised a brow, glancing up at him.

Nicholas smiled, kissing the top of my head. "Not exactly." He set the laptop aside, nestling closer to me as I laid my head across his warm, bare chest. "It's a signet ring—for my family."

"You mean your *violent* family?" I teased.

"Someone's been talking to Angel I see." I giggled as he began to stroke my hair. "She's not wrong. My family is pretty violent." My head tilted up at him as he traced my lower lip. "My family is known as the Saints. We're a powerful family, located all over the world, built of both my blood and well-trusted associates. We control hundreds of clubs—among other...businesses—and have a strong influence over most of the major cities." He really was powerful.

"So you're in the mafia," I teased. Nicholas flashed me a cheeky grin.

"Enough about me," he rolled, carefully laying me on my side as we stared at one another. "How are you feeling?"

I sighed, pulling the silky sheet to my face. "I'm fine." It still felt wrong talking about Theo.

His arms wrapped around, gently pulling me close. "Don't do that. Don't hide from me." Nicholas rotated, positioning himself above me as his hand brushed my cheek. "I want to protect you," his hair tickled the skin of my face as he bent down, whispering into my mouth, "but I *need* to know what's going on in that head of yours."

Our lips met, exchanging a sweet kiss as he pulled back, waiting. My head turned, hesitant to speak. "There's really not much to say." My eyes began to water as I recollected the painful past. "I stumbled into a relationship that turned sour. I made it out, but not before I paid the price. I've been running ever since, too scared to even consider staying in one place too long," my gaze turned to him, "let alone being with someone else."

"I'm not someone else."

I reached my hand up, caressing his chiseled cheek.

"You're right. *You're mine.*"

NICHOLAS

The weather had shifted, a light snow dusting the ground outside, causing me to shiver as I slowly entered the club. The smell of pine and peppermint choked my nostrils as I stepped into a horrific scene. "V," I froze, taking in the main floor of the club, overly decorated for Christmas. "What the fuck did you do?"

V poked his head from around a large Christmas tree, wearing nothing but a pair of velvet green elf pants held up by plastic black overalls and a jingling elf hat, another candy cane in his mouth. "Ah, good ol' Saint Nick has arrived." *God, I hate that nickname.*

"V, I thought we talked about this." I glanced around the club, taking in rows of Christmas lights, tinsel, and mistletoe. "After the shit show of last year's party," I looked at him, "we decided not to go overboard."

V rolled his eyes, "Milo and I discussed it, and you deserve to ring in your birthday with a bang." As the last word rolled from his mouth, he shot off a small confetti cannon, smiling. *I swear, V and his damn dog.*

"Have you seen Vixen?" V glanced back at me, grinning.

"She's with the rest of the dancers, getting ready for the party."

VIXEN

The other dancers and myself had all dressed up in Christmas themed lingerie outfits. I happily adjusted the straps of my Santa set I had put on, matching my vibrant red lips perfectly. Tonight, I would be his Secret Santa.

Music began to play from the main floor of the club, signaling that the party was about to begin. Together, all of us dancers pranced from the dressing room and into the club. Red and green neon spotlights pulsed through the room, strings of multicolored Christmas lights swooping from wall to wall.

"Damn, V really outdid himself this year." Angel chuckled, standing next to me in her emerald green elf set. She looked at me, bumping my arm. "You should've seen the place last year. Fake snow everywhere."

"Sounds like a real winter wonderland," I joked.

"Oh, it was. Pissed Nicholas off real good. Took him weeks to get the club fully cleaned." We giggled together, joining the other dancers and staff at the party. I caught Nicholas's hungry gaze from across the room. He was sitting in a large, tufted, red velvet chair, shirtless, his tattooed chest fully on display, in only a pair of vibrant red Santa pants and overalls. He wore a matching Santa hat, his hair hanging loosely underneath.

V, matching Angel in his elf costume, approached me with a grin. "You should go sit on Santa's lap." He winked. "See if you've been naughty or nice." He pulled a candy cane from his pocket, stuffing it into his mouth before joining Angel. I shook my head, my cheeks blushing as my eyes met Nicholas's. I slowly made my way to him, our eyes locked on one another.

"I hear you've checked your list," I sat on his leg breathing slowly, "so tell me," I leaned in to whisper in his ear, "have I been naughty or nice?"

Nicholas pulled me closer, gliding my hand across the bulge under his pants. "That depends."

"I thought you didn't fuck the dancers, Nicholas?" Candy stepped around the chair dressed in a dark gingerbread outfit, her arms crossed with anger. "I mean, really, Nicholas," she scoffed, "none of us are good enough for you, but this is?" She motioned to me as Nicholas eyed her.

"That's enough, Candy." His arms flexed around me as he fought back his temper.

"No," she bobbed her head, "I think it's pathetic that your standards are so low—breaking your own rules," she glared down at me, "for *damaged goods*." Candy swirled her finger in the direction of my face. Her words stung, hitting their mark.

Nicholas carefully removed me from his lap, then lunged from the chair. Candy's face dropped as she began to stumble back. "I dare you to say one more fucking word." She bumped into V, turning to find him and Angel standing behind her, blocking her path. "This is *my* club," he snarled and she turned to look back at Nicholas, "and she is *mine*."

Candy moved her eyes from Nicholas to myself, "That's fine. We all know you like a good charity case." She looked back to Nicholas, touching her hand on his chest.

"Oh hell no," Angel tried to push past V, but was too slow.

Anger blazed inside as I balled my fist and slammed it hard into Candy's face, knocking her to the floor. The room whooped in excitement, cheering me on as she grabbed at her nose, blood seeping through her fingers. "He did warn you." She stared up at me, tears falling from her eyes. "You should really learn when to shut the fuck up."

Nicholas wrapped his hand around my waist, kissing my neck. "Get the fuck out, Candy."

She crawled to her feet, crying as she stormed away. The room cheered as she left, happy to see her go so the party could continue.

Angel gently hugged me, proud of my actions, as V approached Nicholas, bumping his fist into his chest. "So, when are you going to make her a Saint?" He winked.

Nicholas tightened his hold on me, smiling as our eyes met. "I guess we'll just have to wait and see."

"Alessandra!" The four of us turned to see Theo, his arm in a sling, face butchered and red. He raised his good arm, a gun firmly in hand as he aimed it directly at me. "If I can't have you—" Nicholas slowly pushed me behind his body as Theo finished proclaiming, "no one can!" The gun fired, Nicholas instantly turning to shield me as the room screamed in a panic.

"Val!" Angel's frantic voice cut through the piercing ring in my ears caused by the gunshot.

NICHOLAS

Her eyes stared up into mine, full of panic. Alessandra, my Vixen. I scanned her body, searching for the sign of a gunshot, but she was thankfully untouched. The ringing in my ears drowned out all the commotion around me. Her lips moved, but her voice was distant, buried beneath the sound of my racing heart and heavy breathing.

"Nicholas!" Her voice hit me as she screamed my name. "Turn around!" I spun to find V rising from the floor, one hand on his abdomen as blood streamed down onto his green pants, the other holding Theo's gun. He turned, huffing as he handed me the weapon.

"V," I exhaled. He removed his hand, showing a deep bullet graze. Thank God.

He nodded, patting my shoulder. "I'm okay, boss," he smirked, "going to take a lot more than that to get rid of me."

Angel rushed to V, hugging him tightly as he winced. She then punched him in the shoulder as she scolded him. "Don't you fucking do that again!"

He smiled. "Yes, ma'am."

Theo groaned on the floor pulling my focus back to him. I firmly gripped the gun, stepping directly above Theo. I aimed the gun to his face, watching as fear consumed him. "I warned you."

The Twelfth Day

VIXEN

I could hear his heart beating as I lay across his bare chest. My Nicholas. He stirred, gently waking as he greeted me with a smile, his piercing eyes peeking through his messy hair. "Hello, beautiful."

I smiled back, kissing his chest as I moved to straddle him. "Merry Christmas, Santa," I pulled a small bundle of mistletoe from behind my back, his dress shirt loosely draped around my naked body as I hung it over his head.

"You know," his hands slid around my backside, "it's also my birthday."

I lowered my arm, surprised by his statement. "What? Why didn't you tell me?" He shrugged, rubbing his hands under the shirt and up my back.

"V goes overboard enough, throwing those

ridiculous Christmas Eve parties every year. Hence this," he motioned around the room, highly decorated as Christmas lights wrapped around the four posts of the bed. "With the Saints being so widespread, there's just never really been a reason to stop and celebrate." He smiled. "But now, I have my reason."

"Wait," I raised an eyebrow, "how old are you?"

"32." He leaned his head back, watching my reaction.

"You're only 6 years older than me." I leaned forward the mistletoe in hand, pushing against his chest as I ran the other through his soft black hair. "But I thought I saw a few gray hairs."

Nicholas grabbed my wrist. "If you keep acting naughty, I'm not going to give you your gift." He smacked my backside hard, causing me to gasp with arousal. He rolled us so my back was against the bed as he braced himself above me. His hand ran through my hair, stroking my cheek before kissing me softly. His hand moved, pulling the strand of lights from the post to my left as he slowly unwrapped them. He mimicked his motions on my other side, the two strands hanging from the bed. I flashed him a look of confusion as he lifted my left leg, fully extending it. He pulled the light strand, twisting it around as he placed my hand firmly against my leg, tightening the warm lights as he constricted my hand to my shin. He kissed my leg as he pulled the second strand, tying my other hand to my right leg with a rough delicate touch. "Don't move." Nicholas kissed my center, winking, before leaving the room.

I wiggled my arms and legs, testing the strength of the lights, surprised by how well he had restrained me. I was excited by it all. His steps slowly made their way back into the room as he re-entered, his hand swirling a glass full of ice. He stared down at me, consuming the last few drops of his drink, leaving the ice behind.

"I thought you were getting my gift," I teased as he watched me.

"Naughty girls don't get their gifts first." He picked out a piece of ice, sticking it in his mouth as placed the glass down on the side table and crawled to me. "I'm taking my gift first."

Nicholas held the ice between his teeth as it gently touched the skin of my thigh causing me to shiver. He took his time, gliding the cold cube down my inner thigh as it melted between his lips. His tattooed hands gripped the partially unbuttoned shirt, brutally ripping it apart, groaning as I moaned. He fingered his glass, picking another piece of ice and repeating the motions, sliding up towards my exposed breasts. The warmth of the lights contrasted against the cold ice, sending my body into a frenzy. The ice melted as it neared my nipples, drops of cool water traveling along my flushed, aroused skin.

He placed a new piece of ice in his mouth, rubbing it along my hardened nipples, tracing the shape of me as I leaned into him, arching my back high. I craved his touch. He moved from one breast to the other, giving each equal amount of devotion. As the ice melted, trailing down my sternum, his icy lips brushed my skin, making their way to my mouth. "Do you trust me?"

My eyes met his in a heavy lidded gaze, as I inhaled sharply, "Yes."

The sound of ice moving piqued my interests as he kissed me, a sudden cold sensation inside me causing me to gasp as he devoured my lips. He pushed deeper, rubbing the ice cube back and forth as his palm pressed against me, matching the motion of his fingers inside. His speed and passion increased as my body pulled against the lights, rubbing against his touch.

His fingers moved, feeding the burning release beneath my skin. "I'm going to make you scream my name." He inserted a third finger. "Then everyone will know," he thrust harder, "you're *mine*."

My legs tensed as I squeezed tightly around him, fighting the urge. Nicholas felt my tension. "Oh no, baby, you have no choice." He gripped my nipple with his teeth, piercing me lightly. "Now, come," he growled.

The sensation sent me over the edge as I screamed. "Nicholas!" My voice cracked, the sounds of my pleasure filling the room as my body shook. He continued moving inside me as I soaked his fingers. He refused to let up, overwhelming me with euphoria as my heart raced. "Please," I begged in between moans, unsure if I was begging for him to stop... or continue.

Nicholas's mouth brushed across mine, "Again." His command instantly sent me over the edge, my body fighting the pull of the lights.

As my climax began to fade away, his fingers slowly dropped from inside me as he glanced down at me, clearly pleased with himself. "Your pleasure is mine," he opened his mouth, sucking his fingers with an audible slurp as he slowly pulled them out, "and I want more." I could feel my eyes sparkling with anticipation.

Nicholas gently untied the lights, catching my legs before they dropped. His hands ran down from my knees and towards my hips. He guided my body over as I carefully moved to my knees. Leaning forward, he whispered in my ear, "I know you have more to give me," a sudden rush of pain and pleasure overwhelmed me as he thrust himself deep inside me to the hilt. "Now give it to me." He pulled back, teasing me before impaling me over and over again. My body stretched tightly around him as he slid back and forth, his motion rhythmic, grunting as he quickly began to lose control.

"That's right," I breathed into the air, "fuck me." Nicholas grabbed a handful of my hair, pulling my head back as he pounded into me. The sound of his body ramming into mine mimicked the heavy rhythm of our breathing as we both climaxed, filling the room with our screams.

Our bodies slowly relaxed as Nicholas bent over, kissing my back side. "Merry Christmas, my little Vixen."

"Happy birthday, Nicholas."

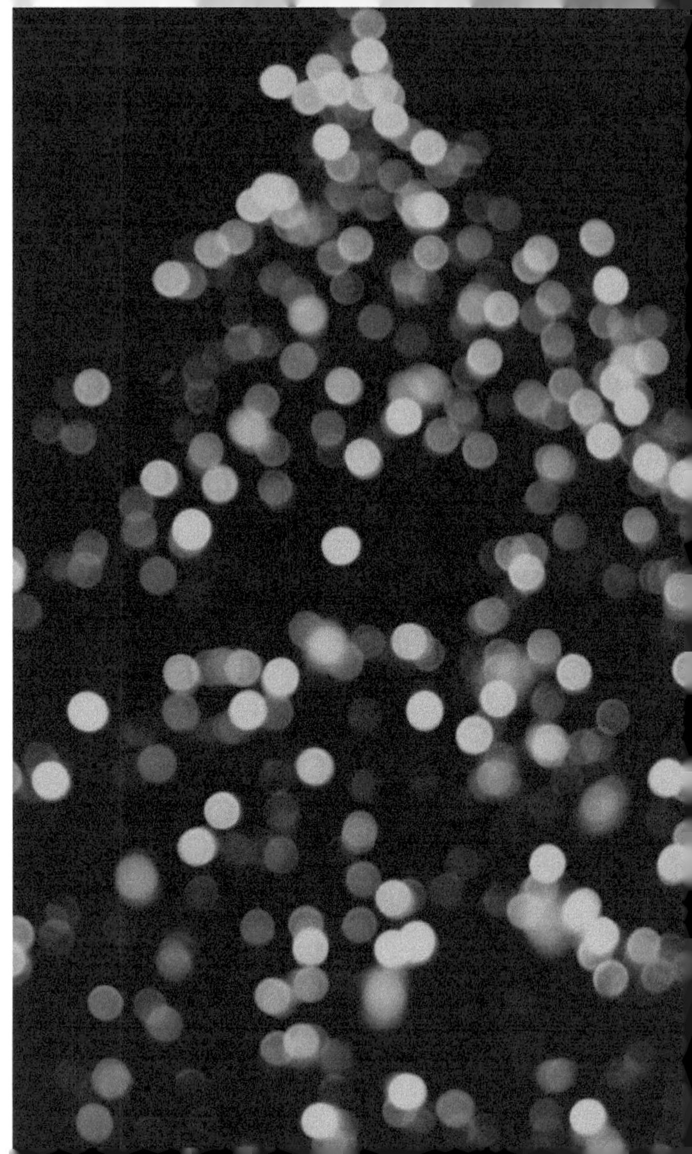

NICHOLAS

Stepping into the main floor of the Velvet Stag, I noticed Vixen seated next to V, Milo perched in his lap as Angel stroked the blonde dog's head. "Really, V?" I scoffed, taking my seat next to Vixen as she squeezed my thigh.

V slammed his hand into his chest, visibly offended. "I took a bullet for your ass," he glanced down, petting his dog. "Milo was almost orphaned." I rolled my eyes. *Dumbass.*

Angel leaned forward, glancing at Vixen "So, Alessandra, huh?" I placed my arm around her shoulder as she nodded. "It fits you."

"Alessandra Saint," V muttered as he pulled a small pink box of candy from his pocket, "has a nice ring to it." He popped a pastel colored candy into his mouth winking.

"Thanks, Cupid," she smiled, "but I prefer Vixen." She turned to me, her tinsel green eyes glistening as they stared into mine. *My Vixen.*

What better way to celebrate a friendship—
and love of all things smutty—
than by writing a spicy novella *together*.